9/19
2e620
21

‖‖ ‖ ‖‖‖‖‖ ‖‖ ‖ ‖‖‖‖‖‖‖ ‖‖
W9-DBI-443

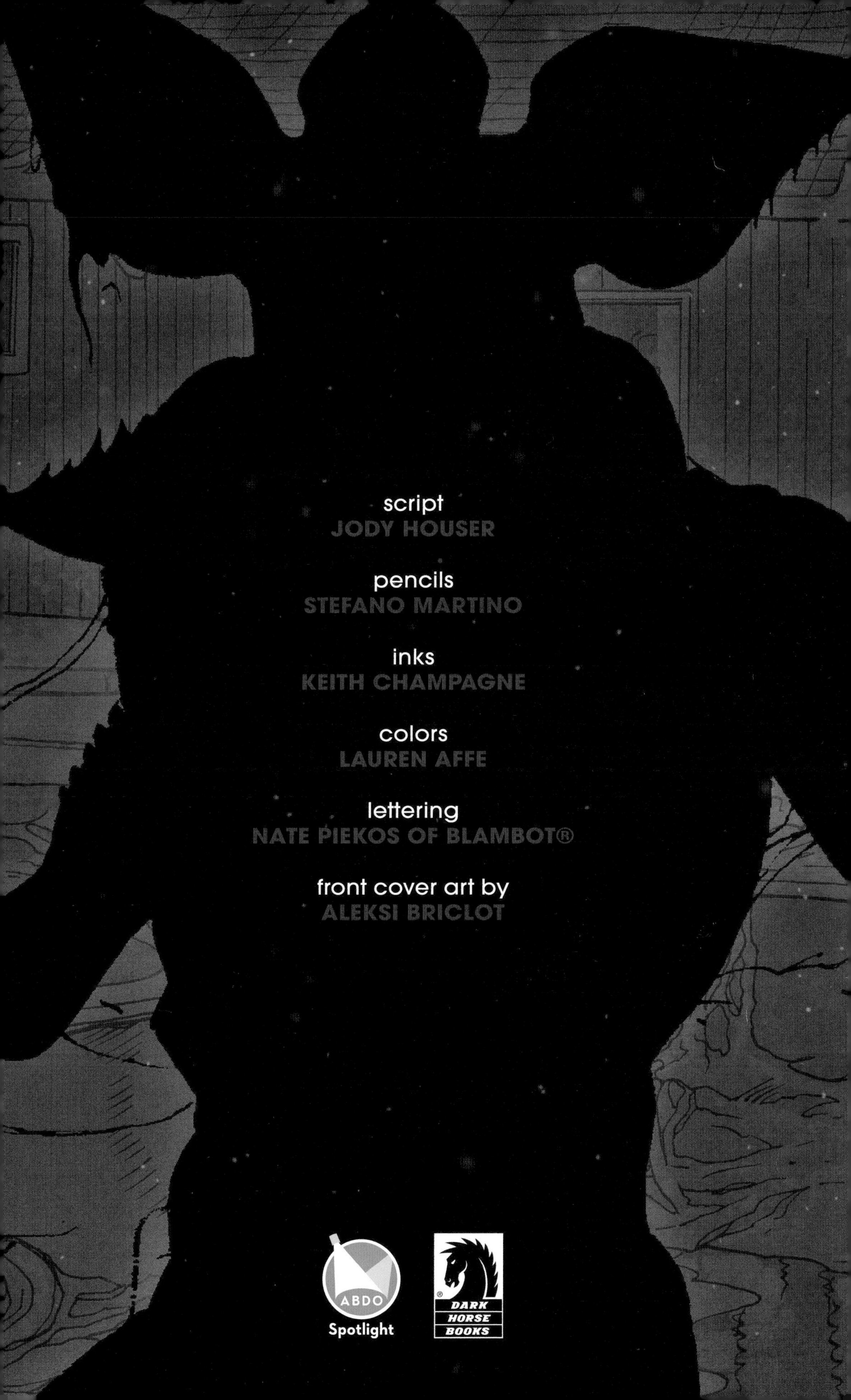

script
JODY HOUSER

pencils
STEFANO MARTINO

inks
KEITH CHAMPAGNE

colors
LAUREN AFFE

lettering
NATE PIEKOS OF BLAMBOT®

front cover art by
ALEKSI BRICLOT

ABDO Spotlight

DARK HORSE BOOKS

ABDOBOOKS.COM

Reinforced library bound edition published in 2020 by Spotlight, a division of ABDO, PO Box 398166, Minneapolis, Minnesota 55439. Spotlight produces high-quality reinforced library bound editions for schools and libraries.
Published by agreement with Dark Horse Comics.

Printed in the United States of America, North Mankato, Minnesota.
042019
092019

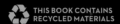

THIS BOOK CONTAINS RECYCLED MATERIALS

DARK HORSE BOOKS

NETFLIX
OFFICIAL MERCHANDISE
©NETFLIX

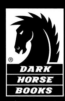

Library of Congress Control Number: 2019939089

Publisher's Cataloging-in-Publication Data

Names: Houser, Jody, author. | Martino, Stefano; Champagne, Keith; Affe, Lauren, illustrators.
Title: The other side / writer: Jody Houser; art: Stefano Martino; Keith Champagne; Lauren Affe.
Description: Minneapolis, Minnesota: Spotlight, 2020 | Series: Stranger things
Summary: This spine-tingling comic based on the hit Netflix series follows Will Byers' struggle to survive in the treacherous Upside Down.
Identifiers: ISBN 9781532143878 (#1; lib. bdg.) | ISBN 9781532143885 (#2; lib. bdg.) | ISBN 9781532143892 (#3; lib. bdg.) | ISBN 9781532143908 (#4; lib. bdg.)
Subjects: LCSH: Stranger things (Television program)--Juvenile fiction. | Science fiction television programs--Juvenile fiction. | Supernatural disappearances--Juvenile fiction. | Monsters--Juvenile fiction. | Graphic novels--Juvenile fiction. | Comic books, strips, etc.--Juvenile fiction
Classification: DDC 741.5--dc2

ABDO
Spotlight

A Division of ABDO
abdobooks.com

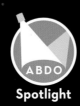

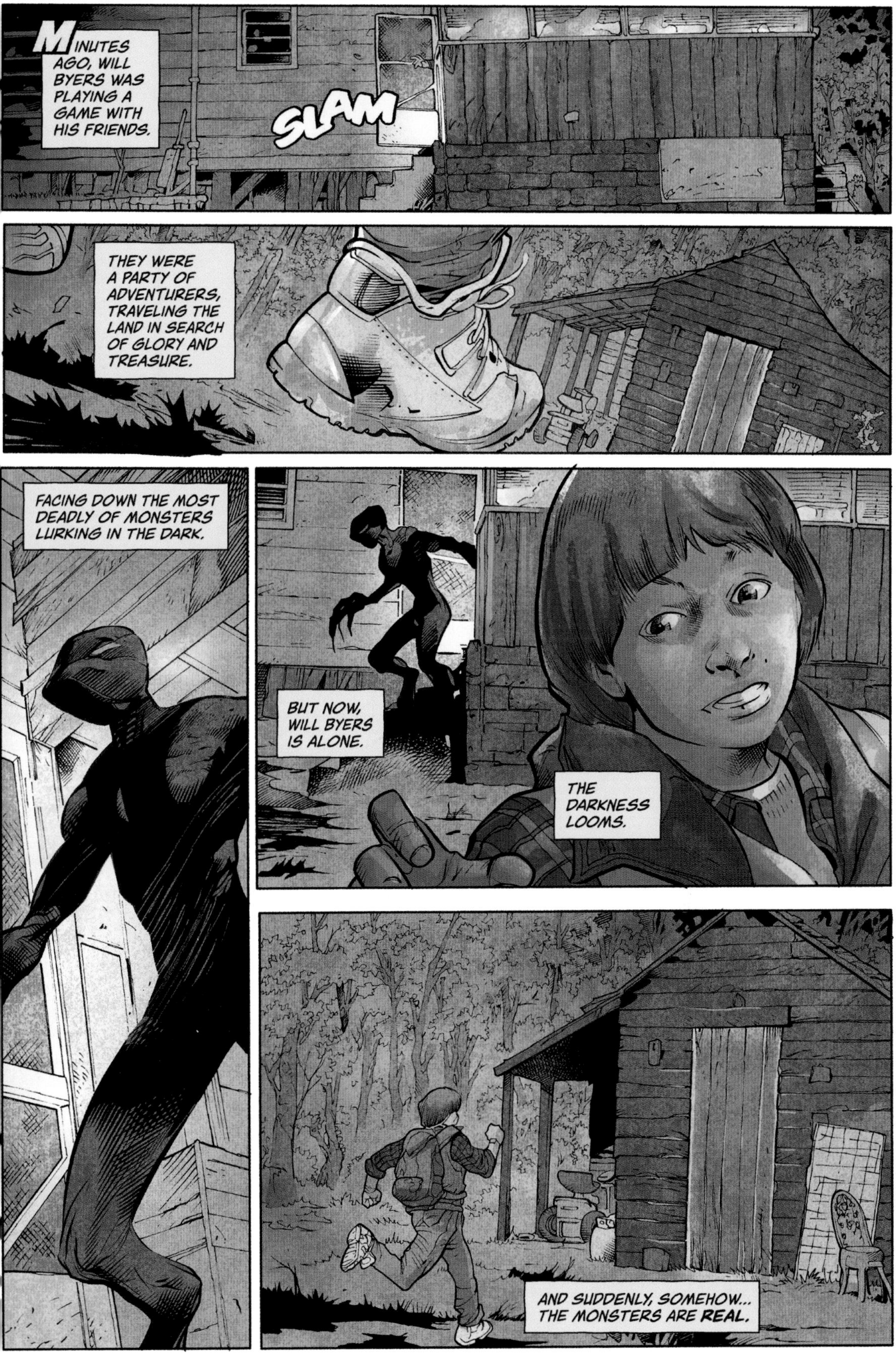
MINUTES AGO, WILL BYERS WAS PLAYING A GAME WITH HIS FRIENDS.
SLAM
THEY WERE A PARTY OF ADVENTURERS, TRAVELING THE LAND IN SEARCH OF GLORY AND TREASURE.
FACING DOWN THE MOST DEADLY OF MONSTERS LURKING IN THE DARK.
BUT NOW, WILL BYERS IS ALONE.
THE DARKNESS LOOMS.
AND SUDDENLY, SOMEHOW... THE MONSTERS ARE REAL.

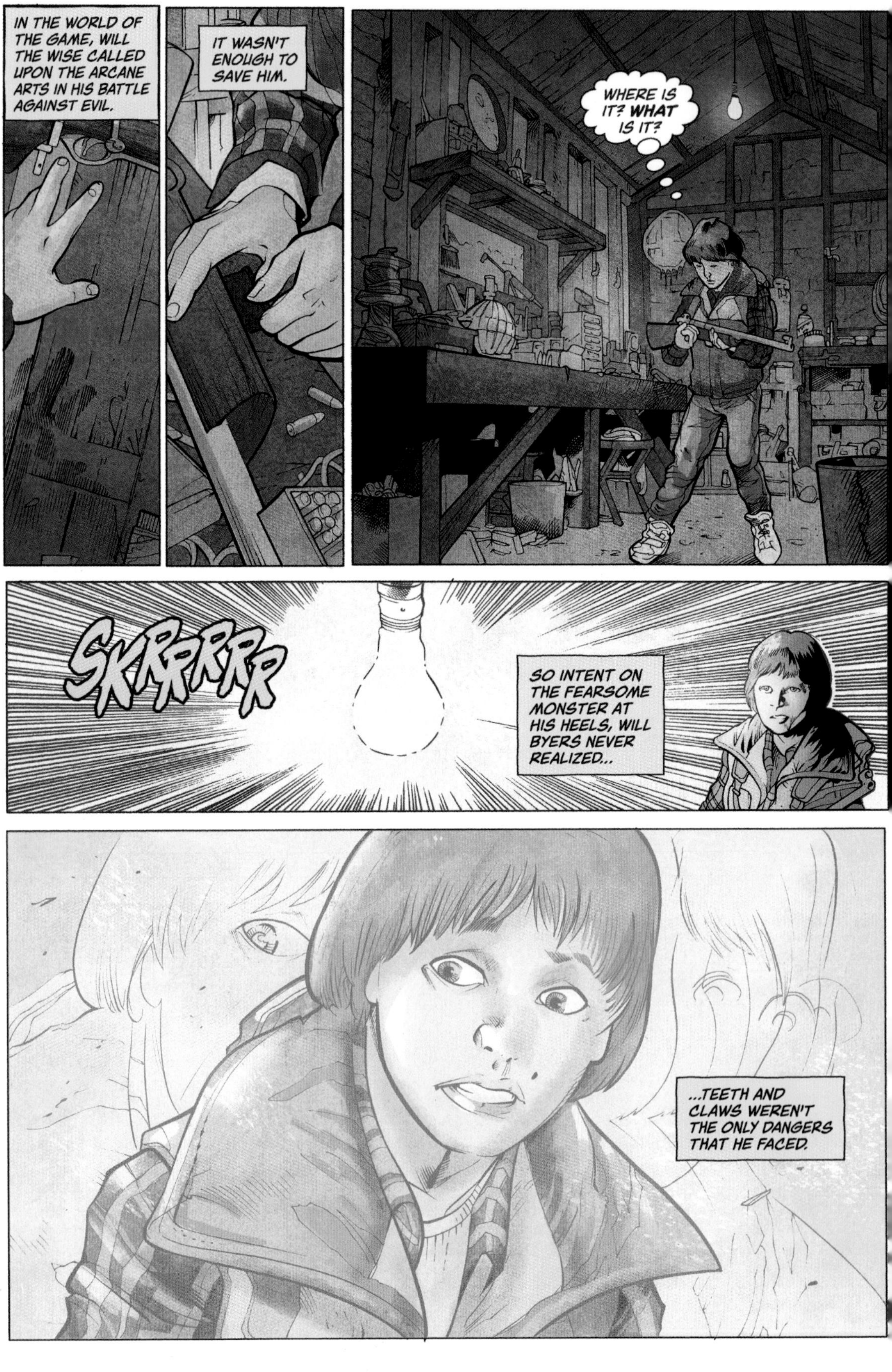
IN THE WORLD OF THE GAME, WILL THE WISE CALLED UPON THE ARCANE ARTS IN HIS BATTLE AGAINST EVIL.
IT WASN'T ENOUGH TO SAVE HIM.
WHERE IS IT? WHAT IS IT?
SKRRRRR
SO INTENT ON THE FEARSOME MONSTER AT HIS HEELS, WILL BYERS NEVER REALIZED...
...TEETH AND CLAWS WEREN'T THE ONLY DANGERS THAT HE FACED.

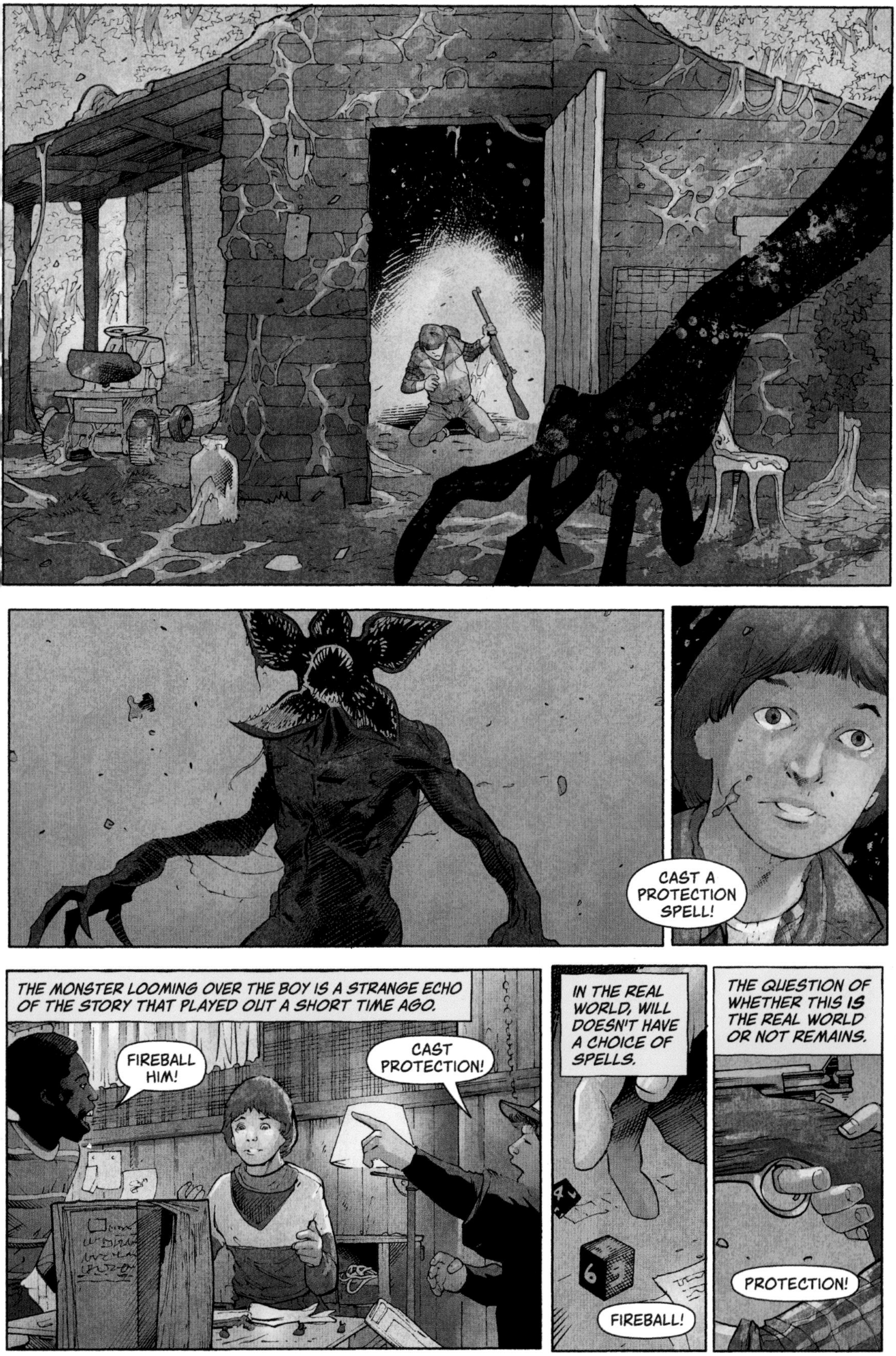
CAST A PROTECTION SPELL!
THE MONSTER LOOMING OVER THE BOY IS A STRANGE ECHO OF THE STORY THAT PLAYED OUT A SHORT TIME AGO.
FIREBALL HIM!
CAST PROTECTION!
IN THE REAL WORLD, WILL DOESN'T HAVE A CHOICE OF SPELLS.
FIREBALL!
THE QUESTION OF WHETHER THIS IS THE REAL WORLD OR NOT REMAINS.
PROTECTION!

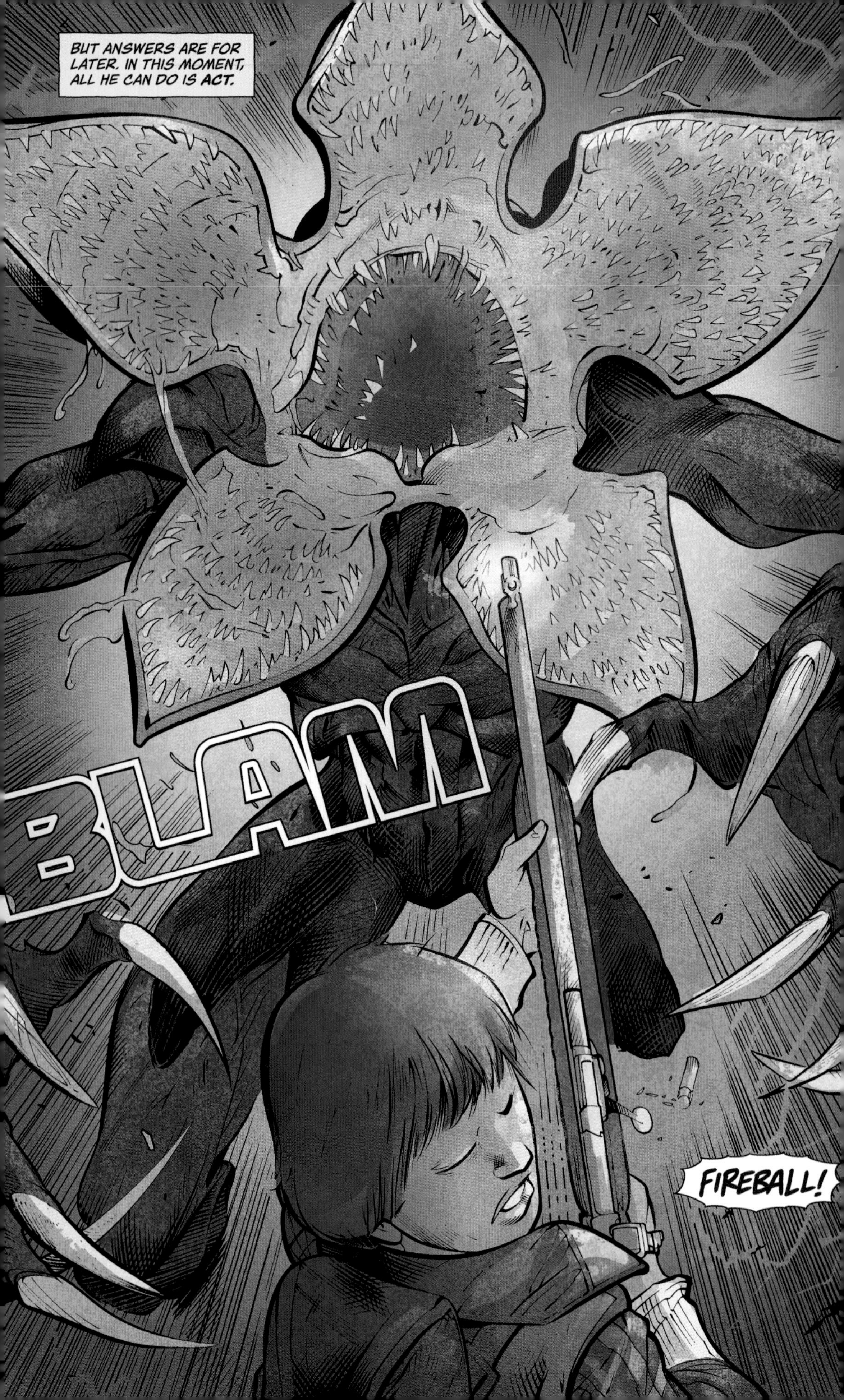
BUT ANSWERS ARE FOR LATER. IN THIS MOMENT, ALL HE CAN DO IS ACT.
BLAM
FIREBALL!

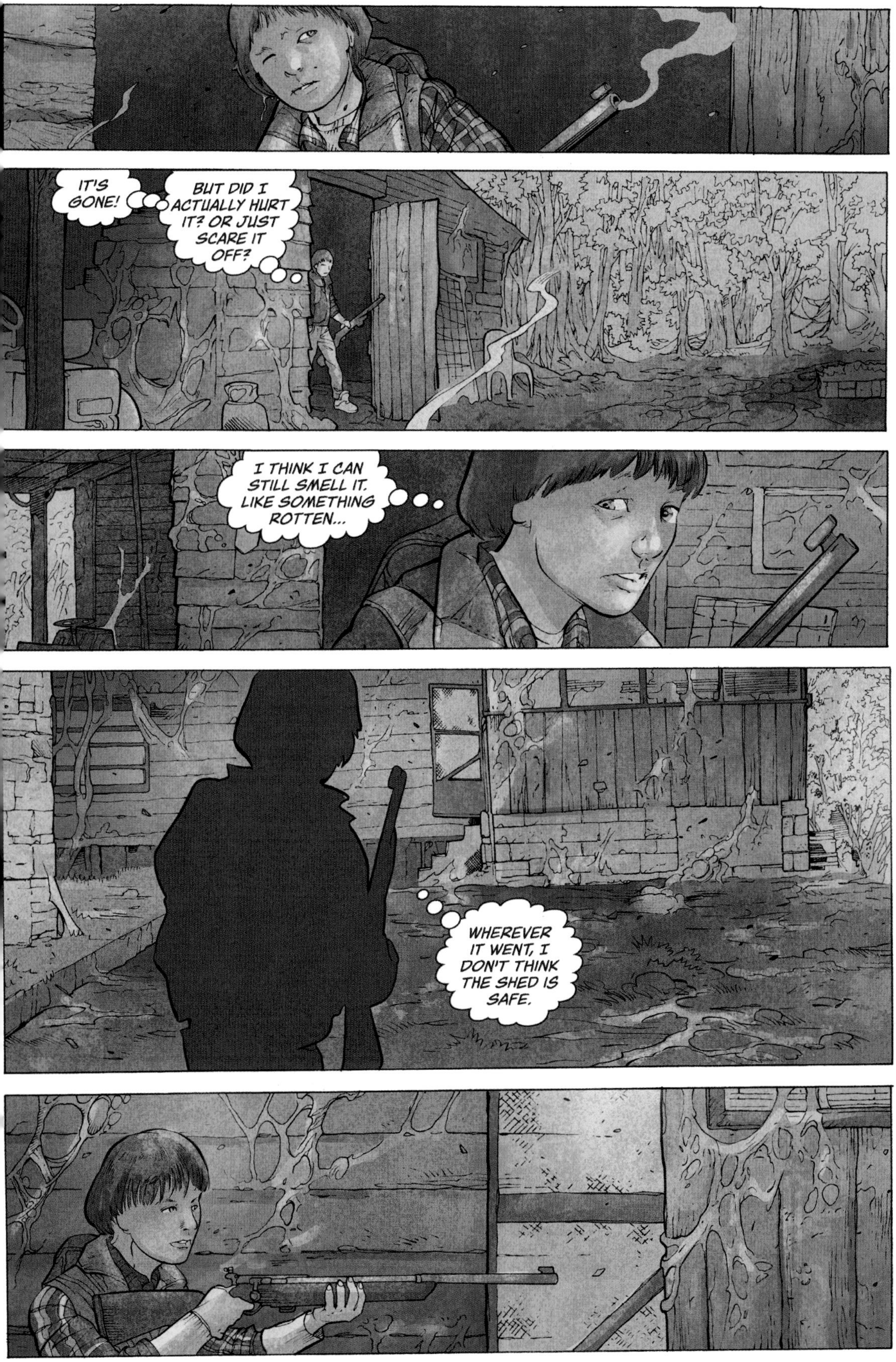

IT'S GONE!
BUT DID I ACTUALLY HURT IT? OR JUST SCARE IT OFF?
I THINK I CAN STILL SMELL IT. LIKE SOMETHING ROTTEN...
WHEREVER IT WENT, I DON'T THINK THE SHED IS SAFE.

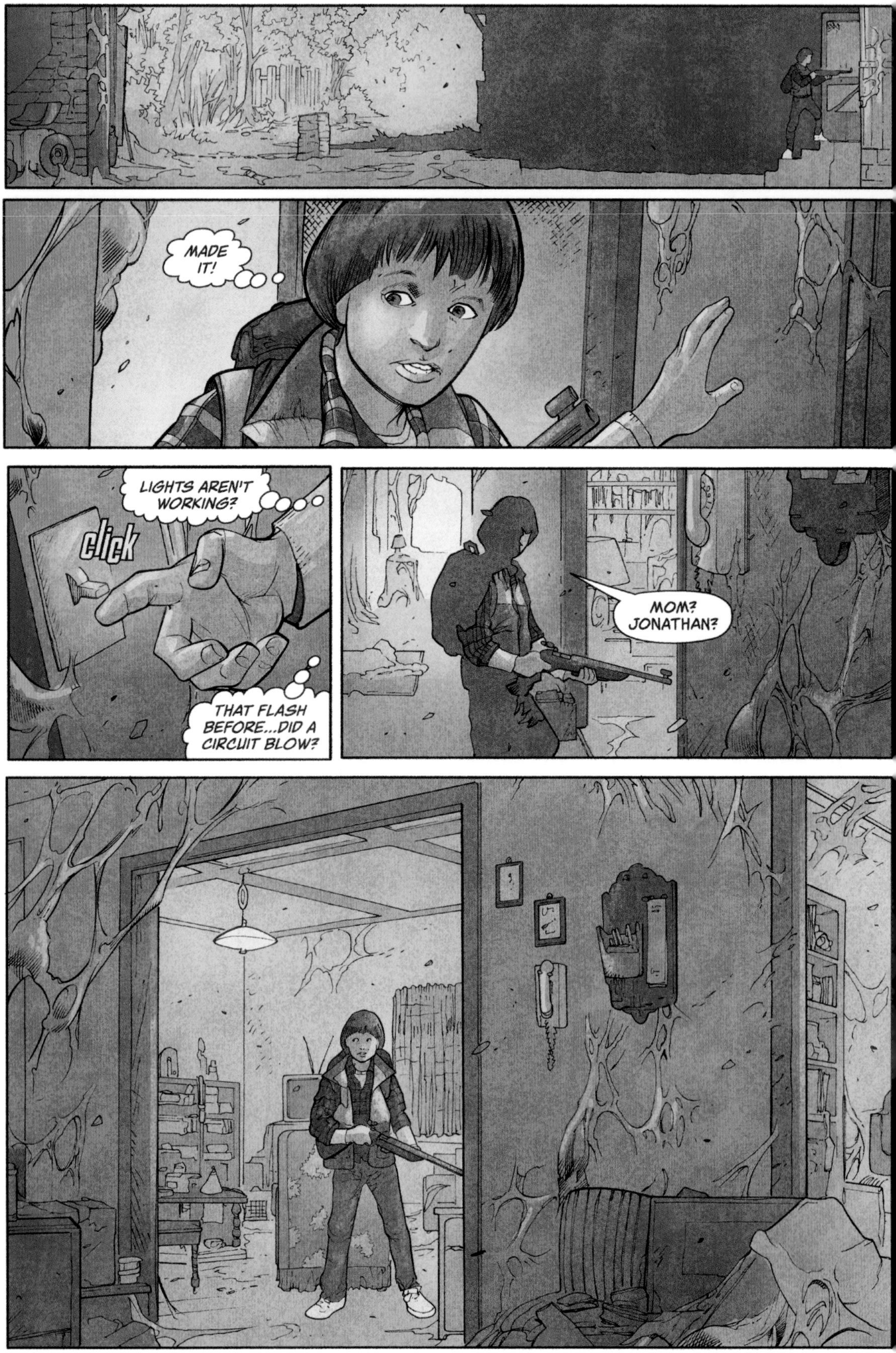
MADE IT!
LIGHTS AREN'T WORKING?
click
THAT FLASH BEFORE...DID A CIRCUIT BLOW?
MOM? JONATHAN?

MOM MUST BE WORKING LATE AGAIN.

AND JONATHAN PROBABLY TOOK HIS CAMERA OUT.

WHATEVER'S GOING ON, THEY'LL KNOW WHAT TO DO WHEN THEY GET HOME.

click

THEY'LL FIND ME.

AS HE WAITS, THE ADRENALINE FROM THE CHASE DRAINS AWAY.

HE MAY NOT YET BE SAFE...

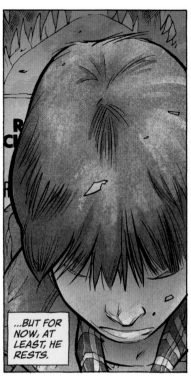

...BUT FOR NOW, AT LEAST, HE RESTS.

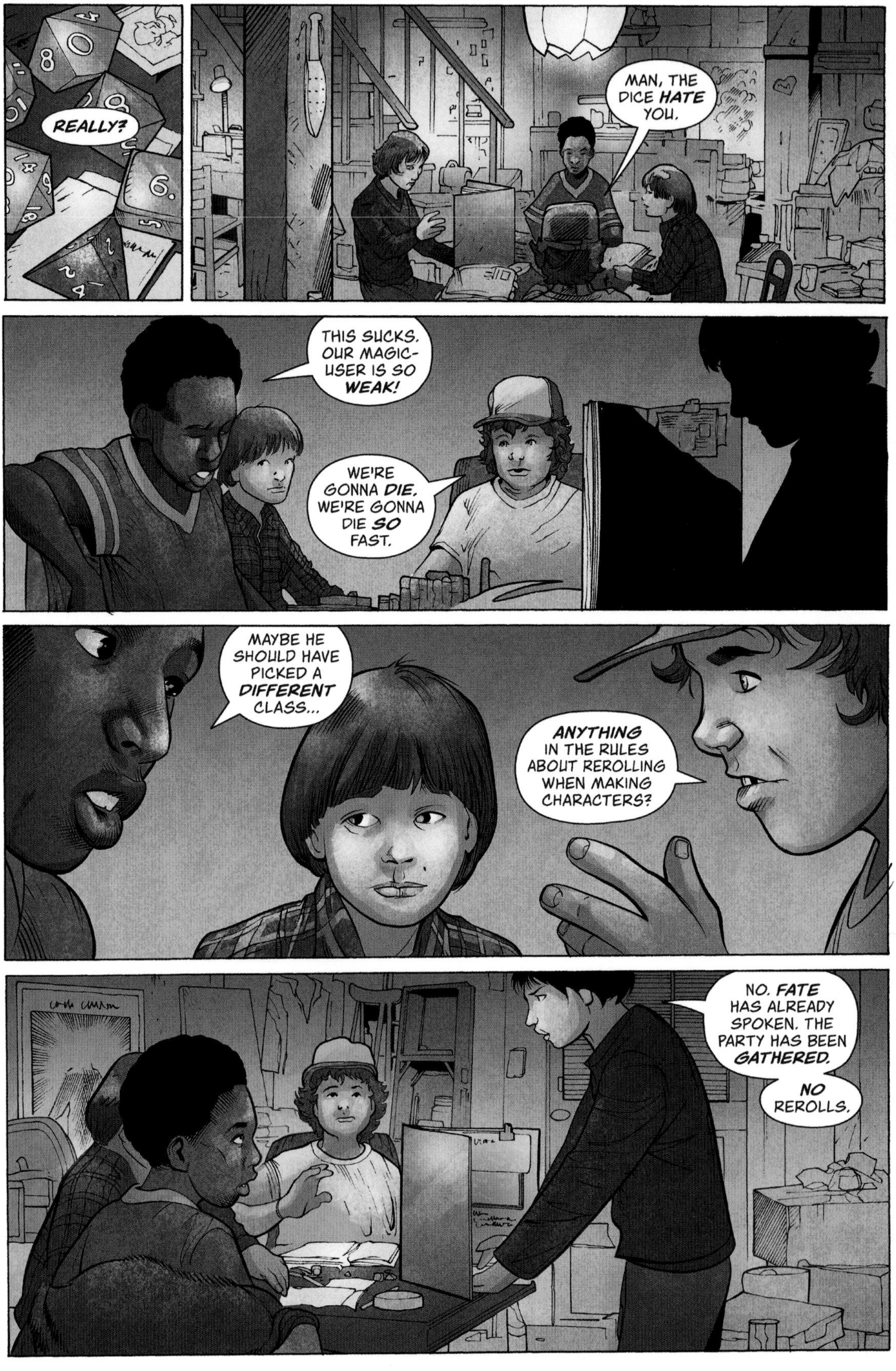
REALLY?
MAN, THE DICE HATE YOU.
THIS SUCKS. OUR MAGIC-USER IS SO WEAK!
WE'RE GONNA DIE. WE'RE GONNA DIE SO FAST.
MAYBE HE SHOULD HAVE PICKED A DIFFERENT CLASS...
ANYTHING IN THE RULES ABOUT REROLLING WHEN MAKING CHARACTERS?
NO. FATE HAS ALREADY SPOKEN. THE PARTY HAS BEEN GATHERED.
NO REROLLS.

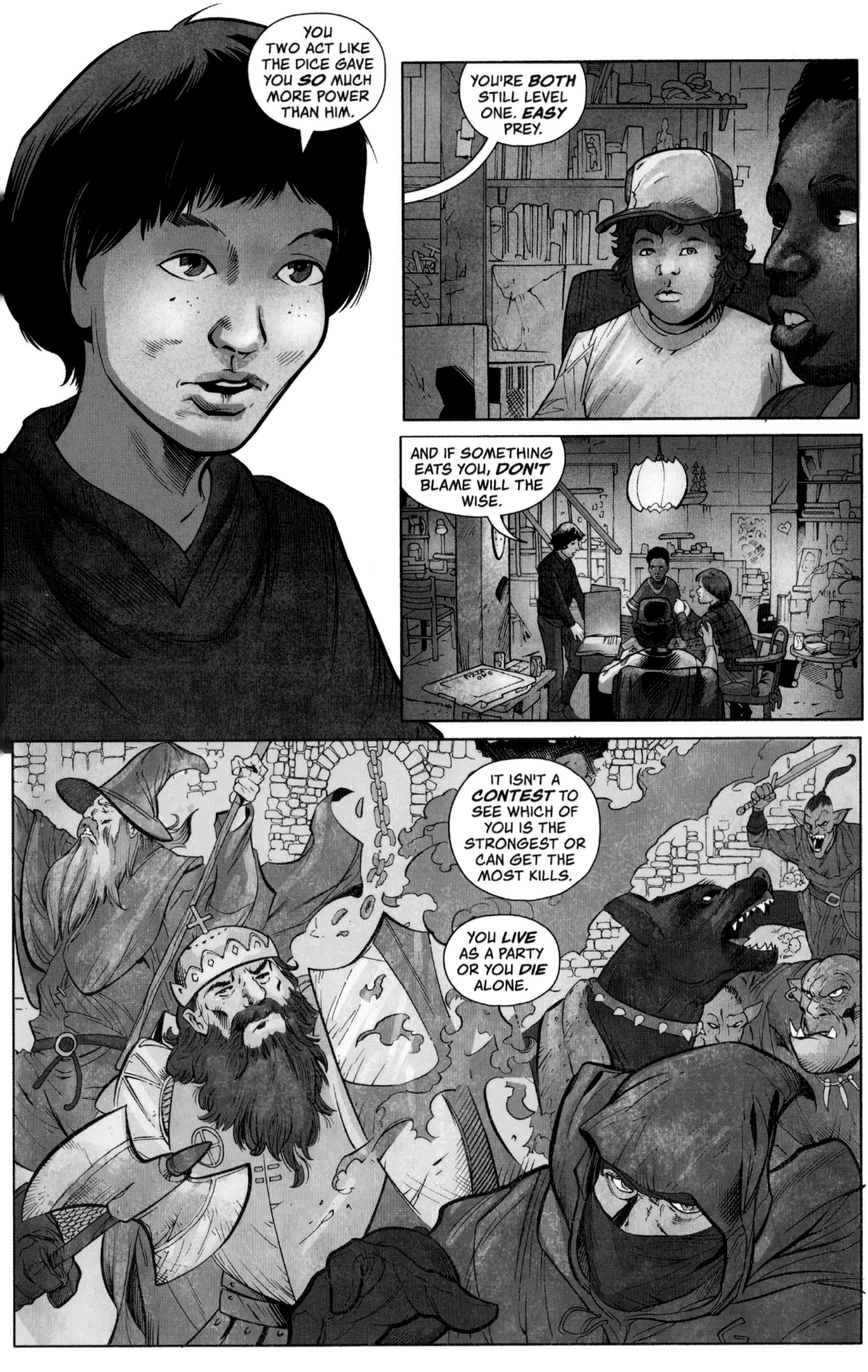
YOU TWO ACT LIKE THE DICE GAVE YOU SO MUCH MORE POWER THAN HIM.
YOU'RE BOTH STILL LEVEL ONE. EASY PREY.
AND IF SOMETHING EATS YOU, DON'T BLAME WILL THE WISE.
IT ISN'T A CONTEST TO SEE WHICH OF YOU IS THE STRONGEST OR CAN GET THE MOST KILLS.
YOU LIVE AS A PARTY OR YOU DIE ALONE.

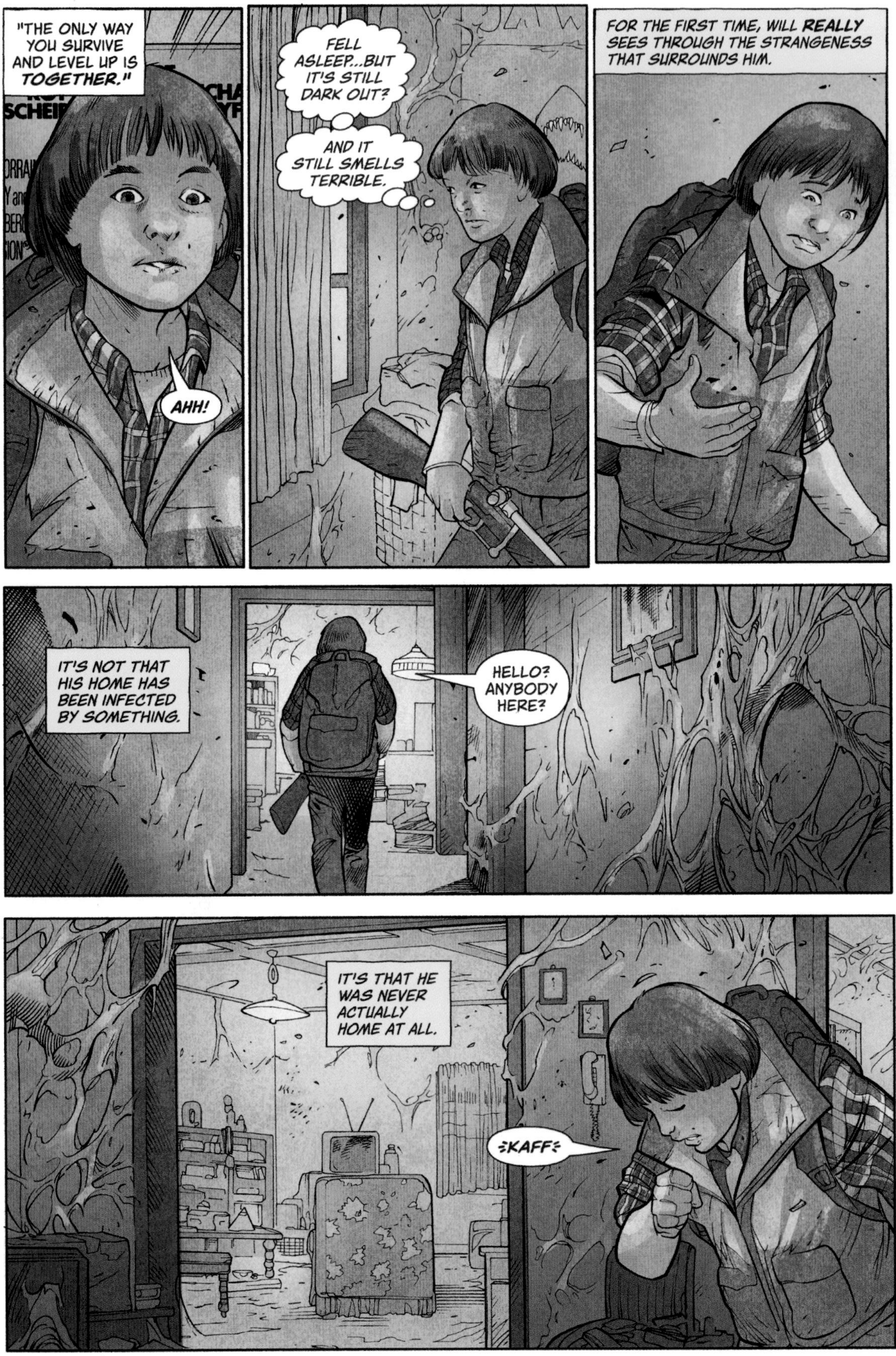
"THE ONLY WAY YOU SURVIVE AND LEVEL UP IS TOGETHER."
AHH!
FELL ASLEEP...BUT IT'S STILL DARK OUT?
AND IT STILL SMELLS TERRIBLE.
FOR THE FIRST TIME, WILL REALLY SEES THROUGH THE STRANGENESS THAT SURROUNDS HIM.
IT'S NOT THAT HIS HOME HAS BEEN INFECTED BY SOMETHING.
HELLO? ANYBODY HERE?
IT'S THAT HE WAS NEVER ACTUALLY HOME AT ALL.
KAFF

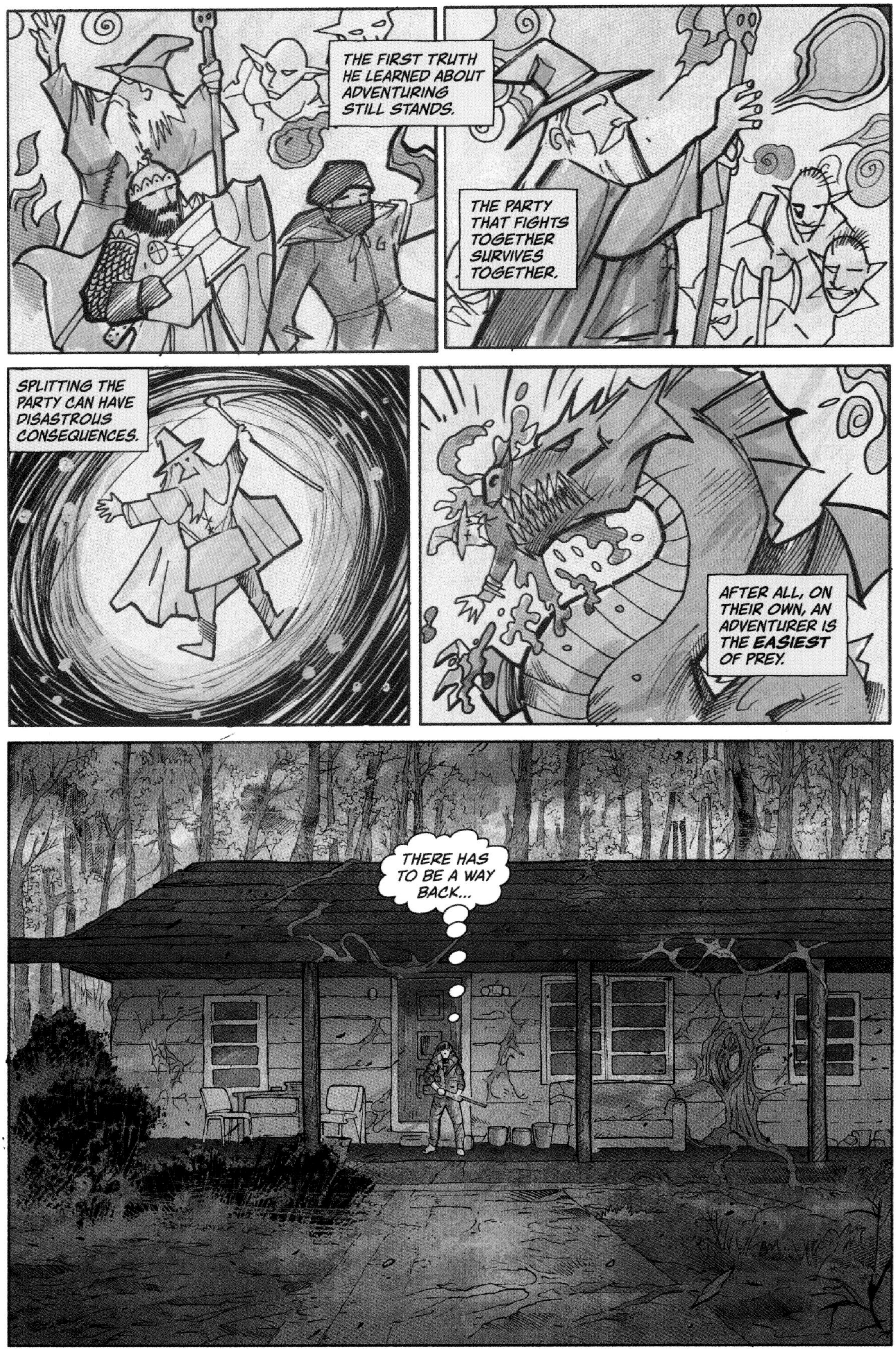
THE FIRST TRUTH HE LEARNED ABOUT ADVENTURING STILL STANDS.
THE PARTY THAT FIGHTS TOGETHER SURVIVES TOGETHER.
SPLITTING THE PARTY CAN HAVE DISASTROUS CONSEQUENCES.
AFTER ALL, ON THEIR OWN, AN ADVENTURER IS THE EASIEST OF PREY.
THERE HAS TO BE A WAY BACK...

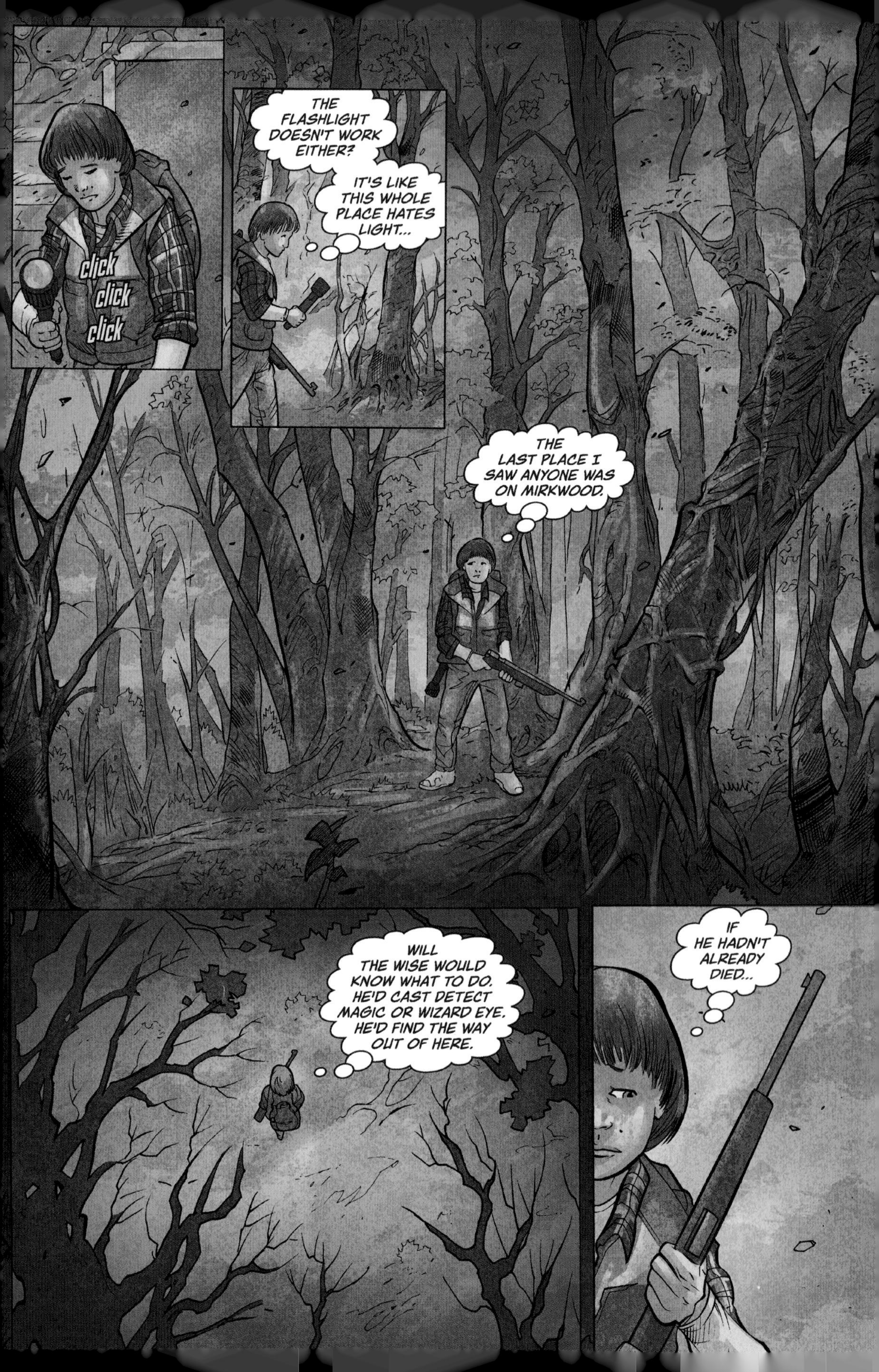
click
click
click
THE FLASHLIGHT DOESN'T WORK EITHER?
IT'S LIKE THIS WHOLE PLACE HATES LIGHT...
THE LAST PLACE I SAW ANYONE WAS ON MIRKWOOD.
WILL THE WISE WOULD KNOW WHAT TO DO. HE'D CAST DETECT MAGIC OR WIZARD EYE. HE'D FIND THE WAY OUT OF HERE.
IF HE HADN'T ALREADY DIED...

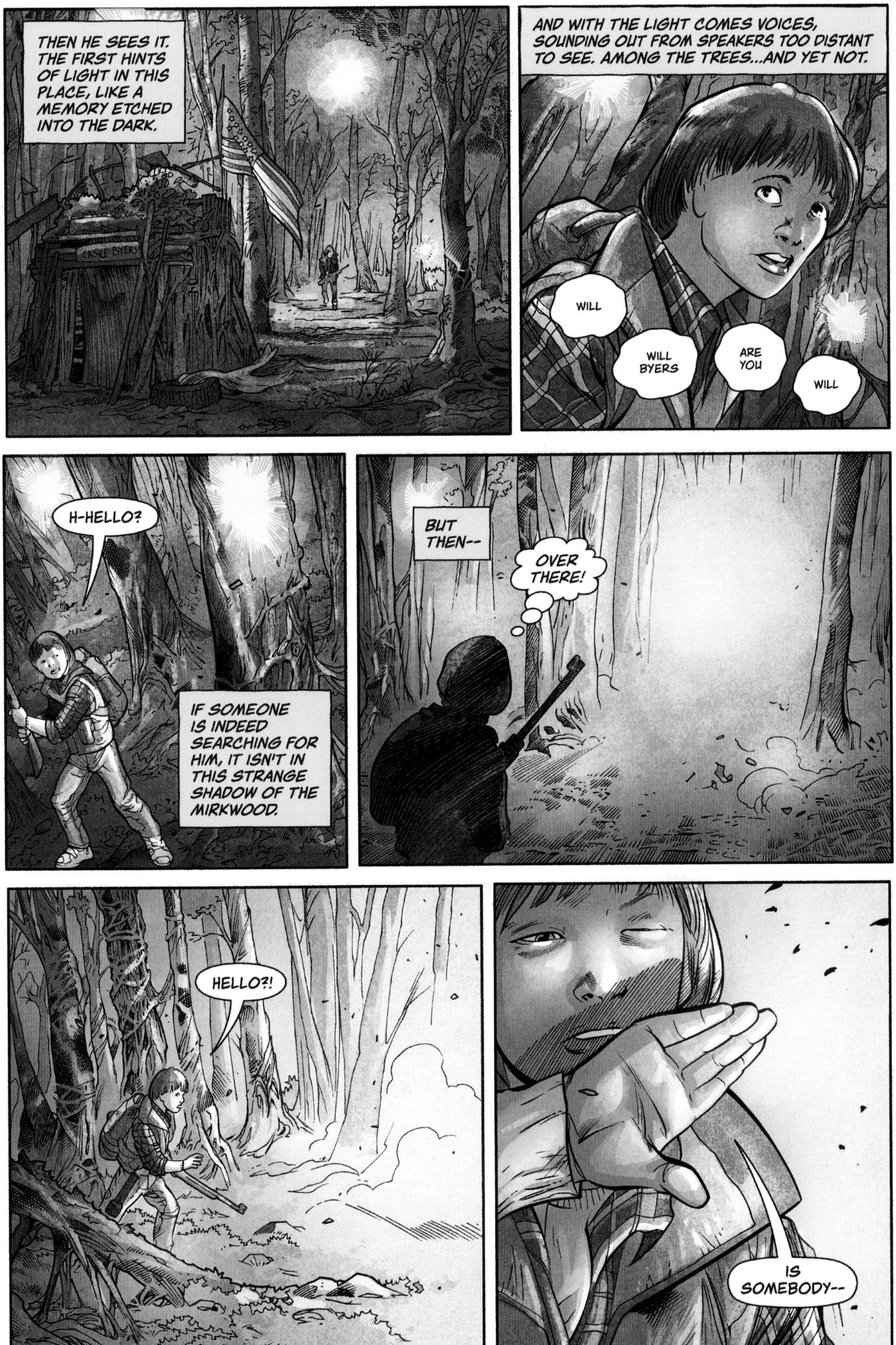
THEN HE SEES IT. THE FIRST HINTS OF LIGHT IN THIS PLACE, LIKE A MEMORY ETCHED INTO THE DARK.
CASTLE BYERS
AND WITH THE LIGHT COMES VOICES, SOUNDING OUT FROM SPEAKERS TOO DISTANT TO SEE. AMONG THE TREES...AND YET NOT.
WILL
WILL BYERS
ARE YOU
WILL
H-HELLO?
IF SOMEONE IS INDEED SEARCHING FOR HIM, IT ISN'T IN THIS STRANGE SHADOW OF THE MIRKWOOD.
BUT THEN--
OVER THERE!
HELLO?!
IS SOMEBODY--

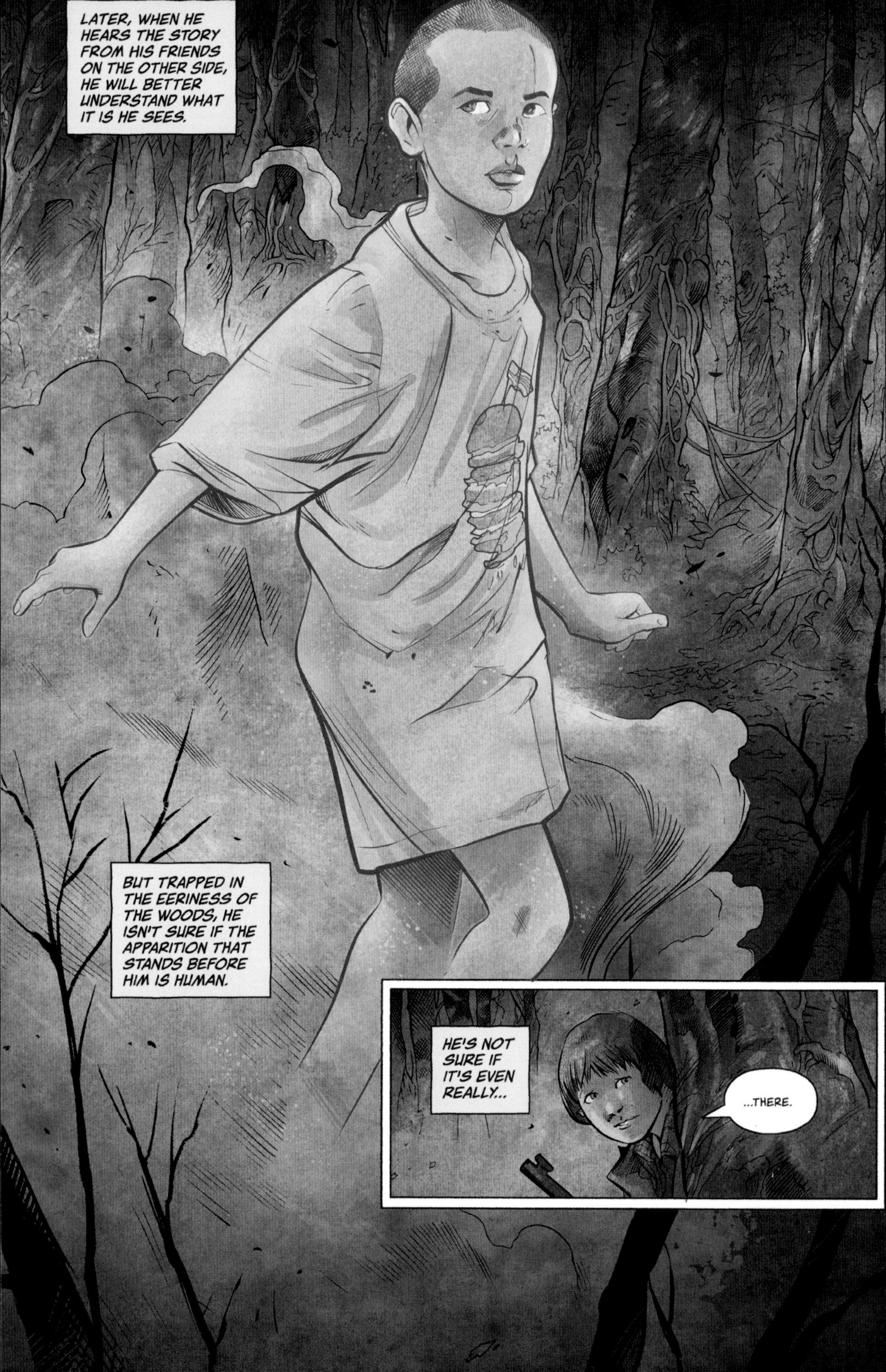
LATER, WHEN HE HEARS THE STORY FROM HIS FRIENDS ON THE OTHER SIDE, HE WILL BETTER UNDERSTAND WHAT IT IS HE SEES.
BUT TRAPPED IN THE EERINESS OF THE WOODS, HE ISN'T SURE IF THE APPARITION THAT STANDS BEFORE HIM IS HUMAN.
HE'S NOT SURE IF IT'S EVEN REALLY...
...THERE.

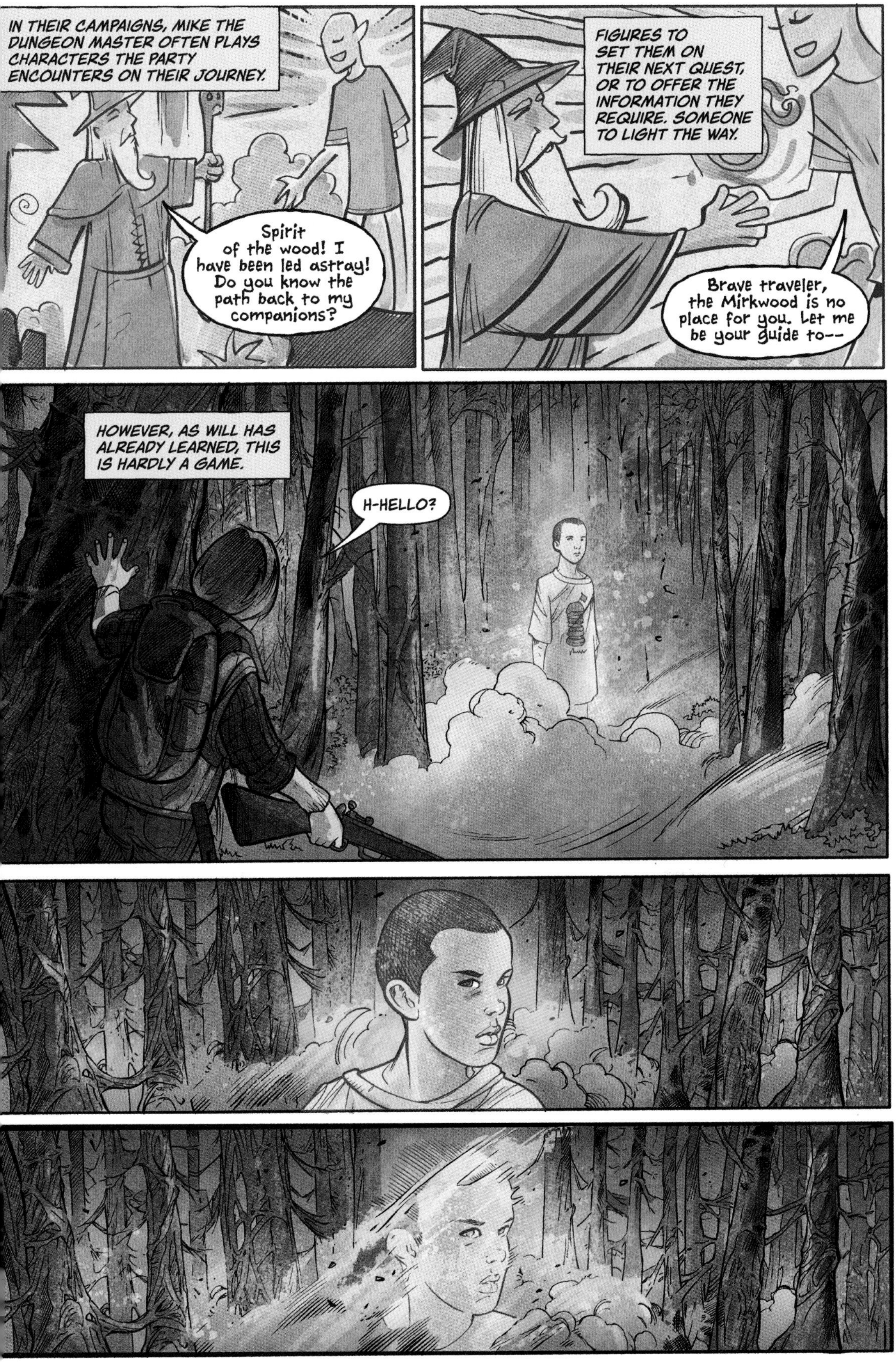
IN THEIR CAMPAIGNS, MIKE THE DUNGEON MASTER OFTEN PLAYS CHARACTERS THE PARTY ENCOUNTERS ON THEIR JOURNEY.
Spirit of the wood! I have been led astray! Do you know the path back to my companions?
FIGURES TO SET THEM ON THEIR NEXT QUEST, OR TO OFFER THE INFORMATION THEY REQUIRE. SOMEONE TO LIGHT THE WAY.
Brave traveler, the Mirkwood is no place for you. Let me be your guide to--
HOWEVER, AS WILL HAS ALREADY LEARNED, THIS IS HARDLY A GAME.
H-HELLO?

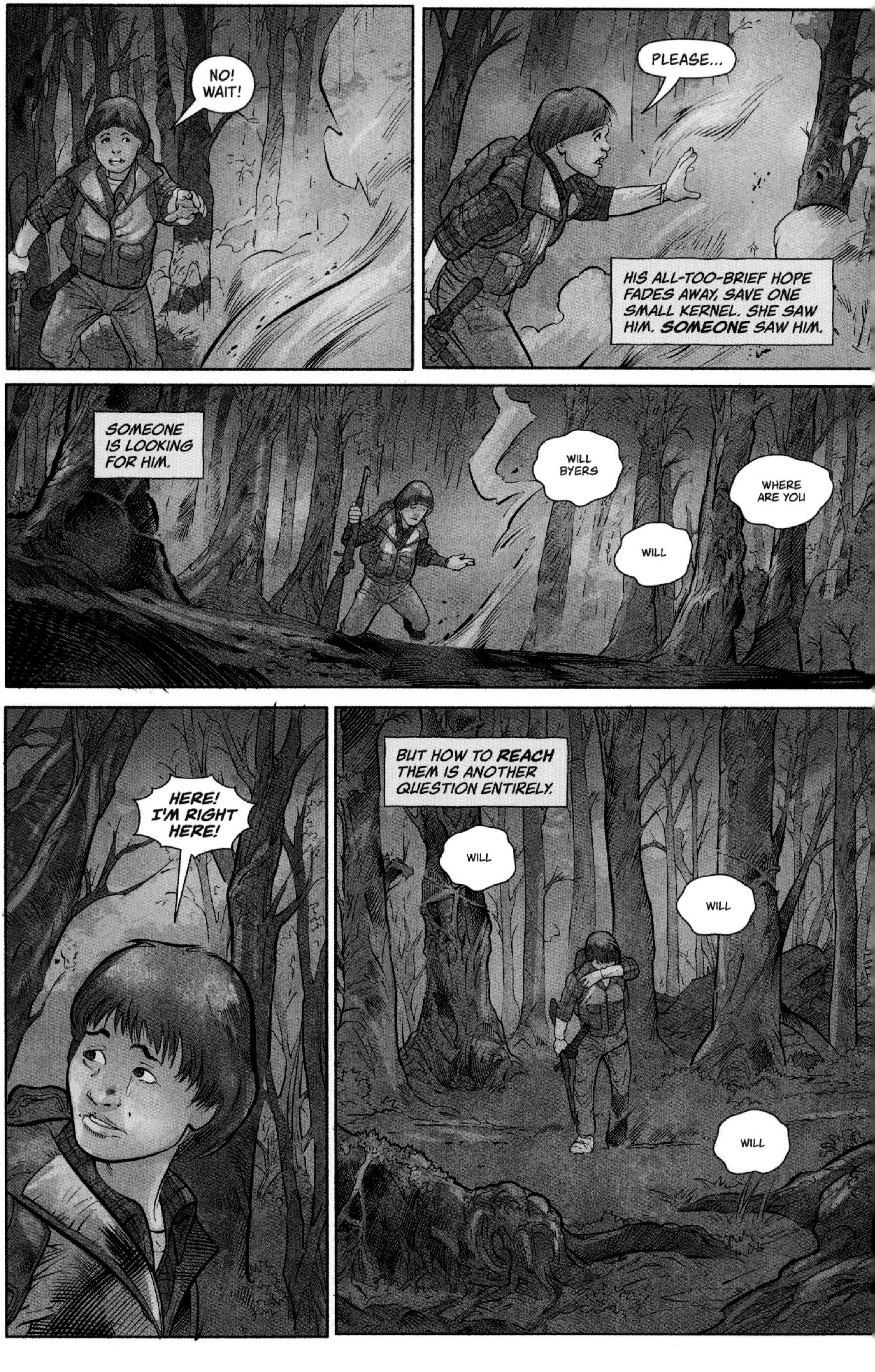
NO! WAIT!
PLEASE...
HIS ALL-TOO-BRIEF HOPE FADES AWAY, SAVE ONE SMALL KERNEL. SHE SAW HIM. **SOMEONE** SAW HIM.
SOMEONE IS LOOKING FOR HIM.
WILL BYERS
WHERE ARE YOU
WILL
HERE! I'M RIGHT HERE!
BUT HOW TO **REACH** THEM IS ANOTHER QUESTION ENTIRELY.
WILL
WILL
WILL

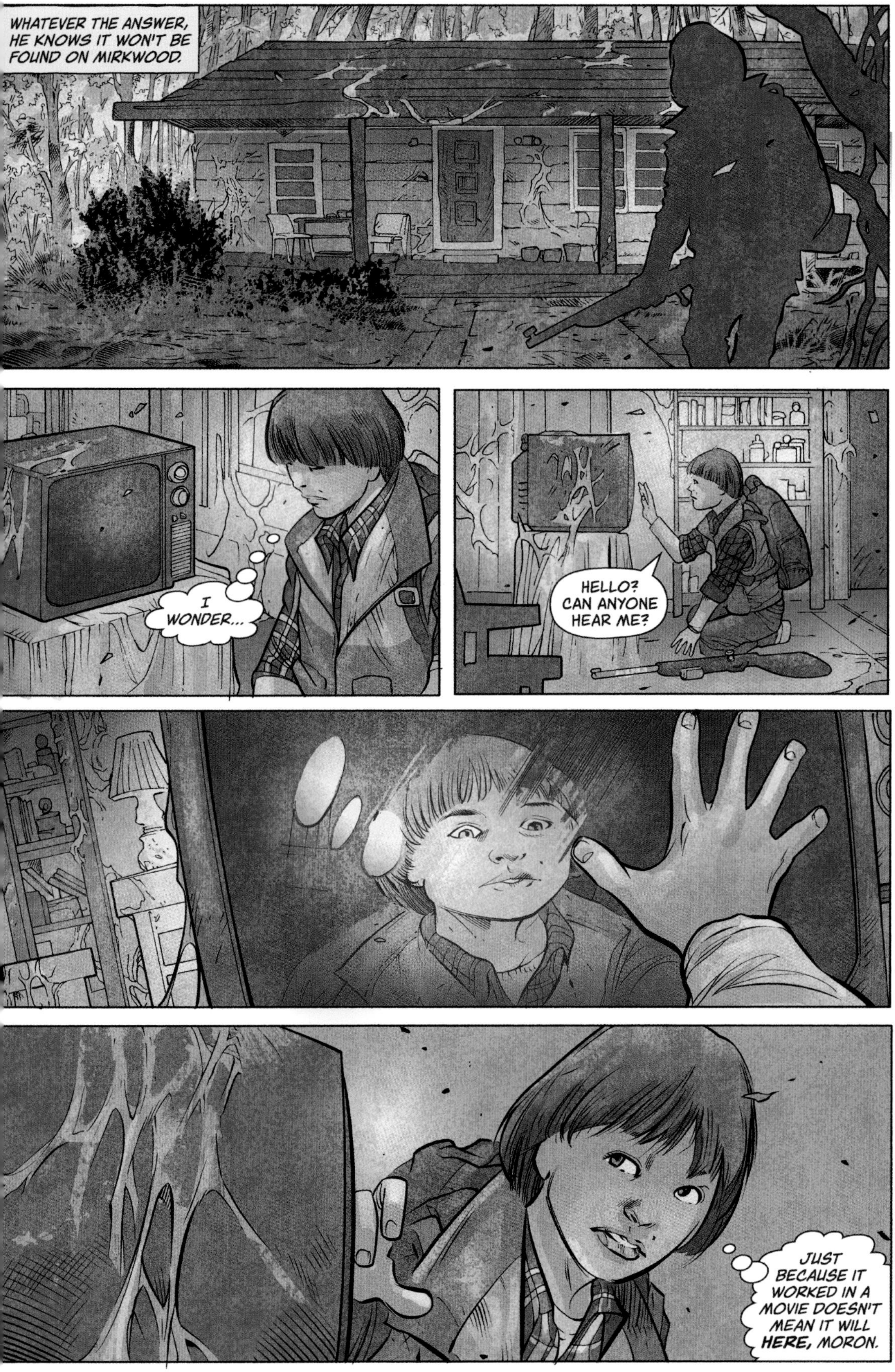
WHATEVER THE ANSWER, HE KNOWS IT WON'T BE FOUND ON MIRKWOOD.
I WONDER...
HELLO? CAN ANYONE HEAR ME?
JUST BECAUSE IT WORKED IN A MOVIE DOESN'T MEAN IT WILL HERE, MORON.

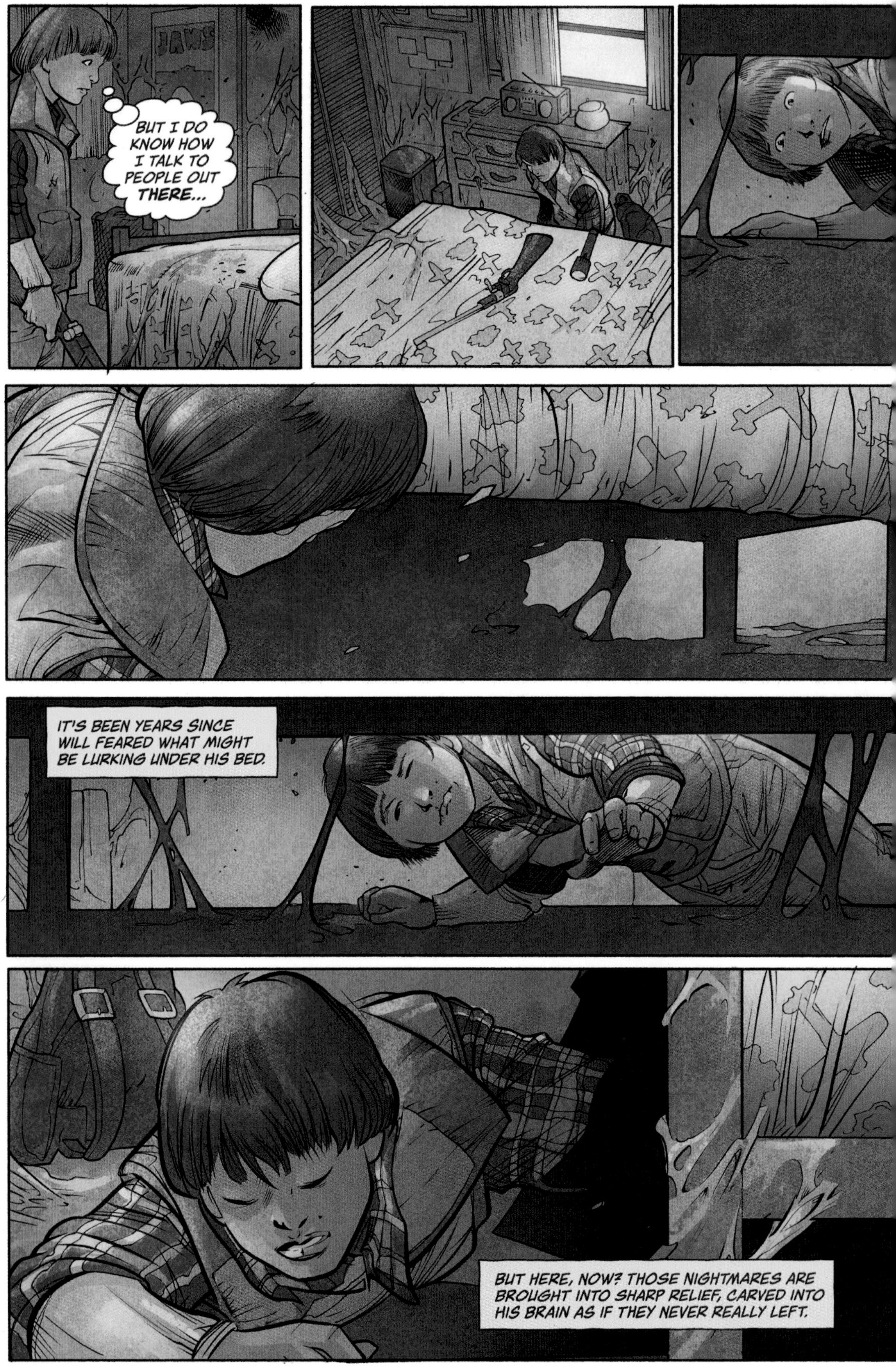
JAWS
BUT I DO KNOW HOW I TALK TO PEOPLE OUT THERE...
IT'S BEEN YEARS SINCE WILL FEARED WHAT MIGHT BE LURKING UNDER HIS BED.
BUT HERE, NOW? THOSE NIGHTMARES ARE BROUGHT INTO SHARP RELIEF, CARVED INTO HIS BRAIN AS IF THEY NEVER REALLY LEFT.

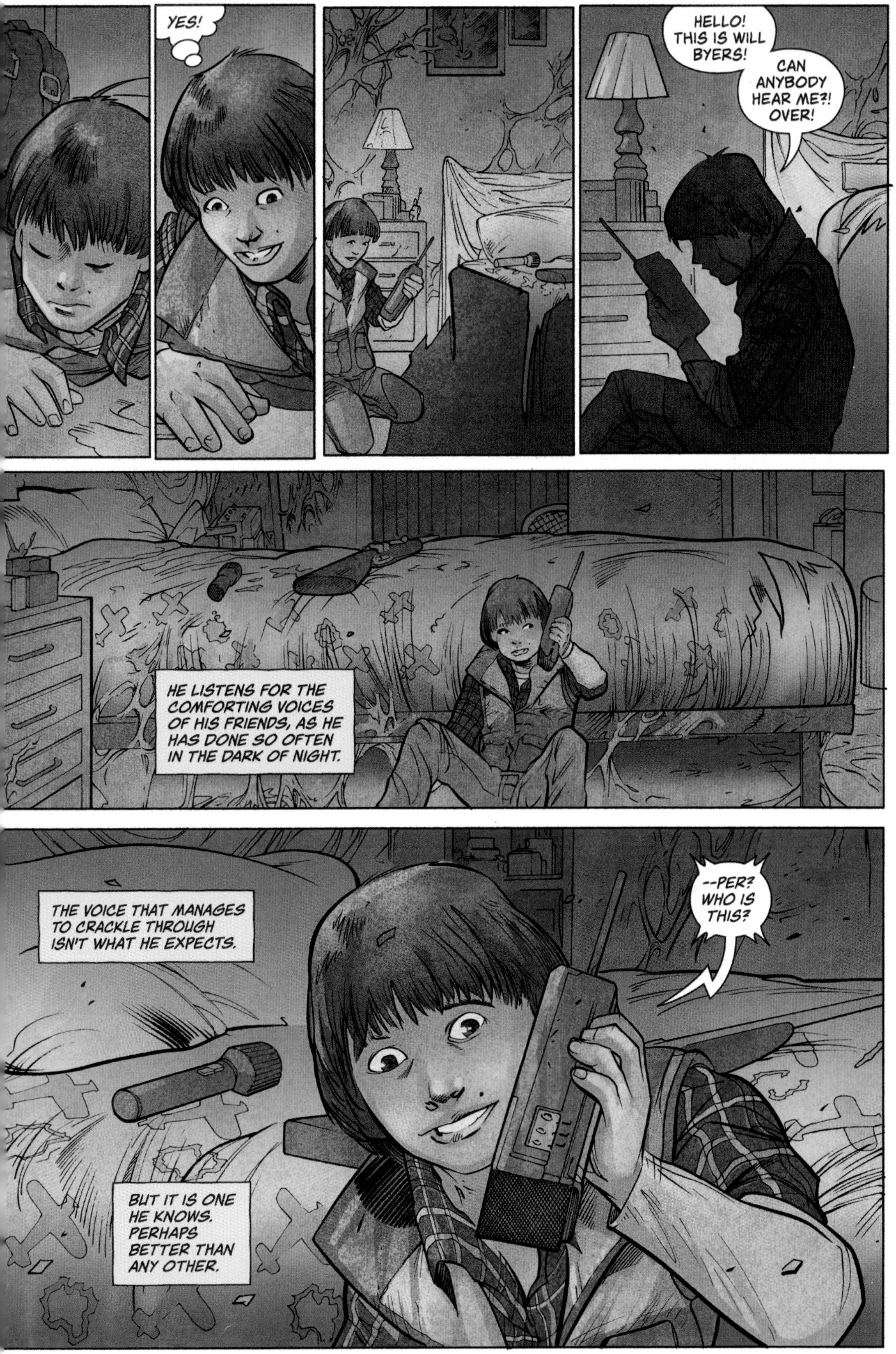
YES!
HELLO! THIS IS WILL BYERS!
CAN ANYBODY HEAR ME?! OVER!
HE LISTENS FOR THE COMFORTING VOICES OF HIS FRIENDS, AS HE HAS DONE SO OFTEN IN THE DARK OF NIGHT.
THE VOICE THAT MANAGES TO CRACKLE THROUGH ISN'T WHAT HE EXPECTS.
--PER? WHO IS THIS?
BUT IT IS ONE HE KNOWS. PERHAPS BETTER THAN ANY OTHER.

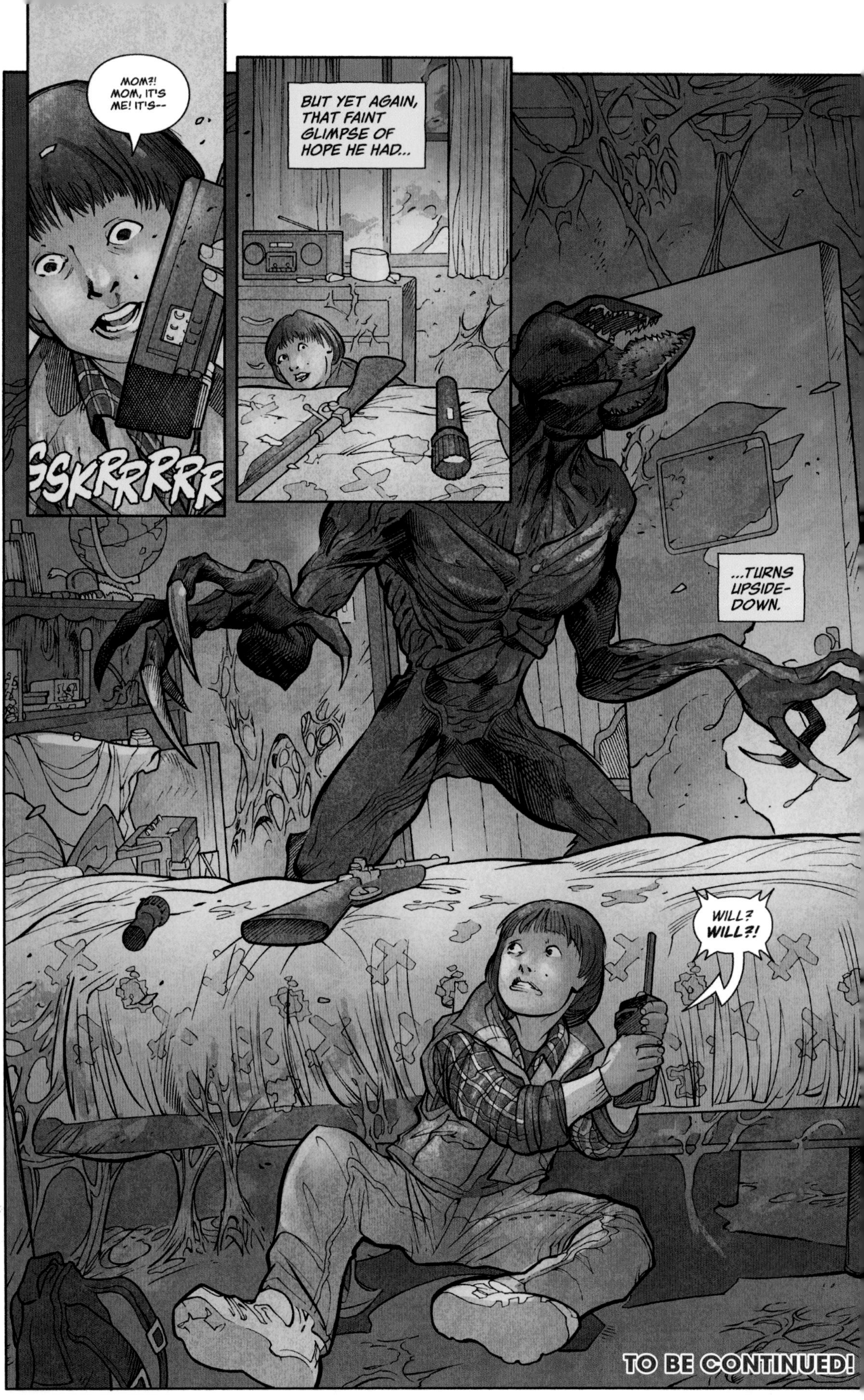
MOM?! MOM, IT'S ME! IT'S--
SSKRRRRRR
BUT YET AGAIN, THAT FAINT GLIMPSE OF HOPE HE HAD...
...TURNS UPSIDE-DOWN.
WILL? WILL?!
TO BE CONTINUED!